TWISTED LIBRARY
VOLUME 2

SHORT HORROR STORIES ANTHOLOGY

BRYCE NEALHAM

Copyright © Bryce Nealham.

All Right Reserved.

No part of this publication may be reproduced, distributed, or transmitted in any form or by any means, including photocopying, recording, or other electronic or mechanical methods, or by any information storage and retrieval system without the prior written permission of the publisher, except in the case of very brief quotations embodied in critical reviews and certain other noncommercial uses permitted by copyright law.

MORE BOOKS FROM THIS AUTHOR

CONTENTS

STORY 1 1
   Acid Funhouse 1

STORY 2 11
   The Telepath 11

STORY 3 21
   Half 21

STORY 4 35
   Strangled 35

STORY 5 45
   We All Have Secrets 45

STORY 6 57
   Filthy Rich Bloodsuckers 57

STORY 7 67
   Wormwalkers 67

STORY 8 77
   The Living Room 77

STORY 9 87
   The Red Room 87

STORY 1
Acid Funhouse

"This is it, this is the last place Sally visited before she went missing." Ben pointed out to his friends.

"She came here for a Halloween party last year and she never came home." Ben was in his first year of studying to be a pilot, he'd deferred when his sister went missing but was in a better place to study and search for her now.

The trio stood in front of a large warehouse in a remote industrial area, the large building was the size of a department store. It was run down and would have looked abandoned if it wasn't for the three men out the front who were dressed in strange costumes.

There was also a stall selling vodka and foul smelling treats and strange over-sized lollipops that had nasty colors that looked far from pleasant.

On a closer inspection here was violent imagery painted on the entrance of the door, images of humans being eaten alive. The windows were all boarded up and there were a group of strange people in clown costumes out the front who were leering at them and laughing

"Ben, can't we just call the police on these weirdos? I mean, this place just feels evil and those people look dodgy." Nathan piped up. Nathan was in his first year of medicine and was the most reasonable one.

"Don't be a wimp Nathan, let's find Sally and take these clowns down." Kyle flunked college and decided to take up a boxing career instead. "See, I can take these steroid fueled creeps."

"You guys seen my sister? She came to this exact place for your Halloween party this time last year and she never came home. You were posting last year's event all over social media, why not this time? What are you hiding?" Ben confronted the largest member who reeked of vodka and was stuffing his face with what looked like pork as he chewed with his mouth open.

The three clowns blocking the entrance wore colorful and bright costumes with offensive patterns that did not look right. One of them had glittery and flashing lights wrapped around his bizarre costume, the large one had war paint make up and was eating pork balls and the third was muscular and only wore a skimpy pink tutu. The third one in particular seemed to offend Kyle who was itching for a fight.

"You're welcome into our house and look for her, our house will eat you right up. Maybe I am eating your sister right now." The biggest clown started to eat his pork obnoxiously and Ben started to feel nausea when he realized the pork balls the clown was eating had hair sticking out.

"You sicko!! The hell would you say that? Who are you all? Bunch of pedos?" Kyle took a menacing step towards the largest clown but Nathan held him back.

"Kyle, calm down. Let's call the police." Nathan positioned himself between his friends and the strange clown men. "Shut these creeps down before anyone else gets hurt. C'mon. Let's get out of this hole."

"Don't you want to find Sally? She's still in there Ben. Little Sally is waiting for you, she would be so proud of you. Are you going to be a brave little pilot and save her?"

"How do you know her name? Or my name? Or anything? How do you know?" Ben shouted. "Guys they wouldn't know me unless Sally told them which means she is alive and waiting for me, right?" Ben knew this trio knew too much, they seemed to know about him and they would only know if Sally had told them about him.

"Ben!! He can find that information online. Please, let's just get out of here and call the police." Nathan pleaded and his eyes widened as Tutu Clown snatched his phone and threw it hard against the wall. Predictably that triggered Kyle to throw a punch at Tutu clown who dodged and easily shoved Kyle onto the gravel.

"You're welcome inside, we are having a huge party and looking after Sally so well. We aren't holding her against her will, come inside if you like." The clown with the flashing lights put a hand on Bens shoulder, and Ben winced as the man smelt as if he hadn't washed in days. "One condition though, you gotta take some candy first to really enjoy the experience."

"Ben, if you take that-" Nathan started but in horror he watched as Ben simply swallowed the candy and headed inside. "Ben wait!!No!!!!"

Kyle stood next to Nathan now as the two young men squared up against the sinister trio. "Get outta the way!!" The men simply laughed and held up two large dirty looking syringes with a sparkly bright green substance inside of it and moved towards the young adults threateningly.

"You gonna join your friend or should we forcibly inject you? You should know, if you move too much we may accidental kill you from an overdose. You gonna let your friend die alone or do you want to join him in there? Secret is. No one makes it out alive; we stream this stuff to the dark web for some Ka-Ching."

The two young men turned to run but Tutu Clown grabbed them both in a headlock, the two men struggled to get free. "You both had your tetanus shots? Our needles aren't sanitary. These aren't single use needles and we don't wash them. You'll probably get all kinds of nasty diseases to remember this experience by, fun right?"

The largest clown forcibly injected them both with the green sparkling liquid and Nathan and Kyle winced from the sharp jab of the needle. If they lived through the night they were going to need to seek urgent medical attention from a needle stick injury and whatever they have been injected with. "You're both going inside that house. Move!!!"

Nathan and Kyle yelped as they were both thrown into the house, landing on Ben who collapsed shortly after walking into the house. Ben was frothing at the mouth and spitting the toxic substance as he was clearly already affected by the drug. They were in a tiny room with nasty red flashing lights and a siren that was obnoxiously loud and was sounding as if to warn them to vacate the building.

"Those crazy fucks, what the hell have they given us! What was in that syringe? Do you know how many viruses we can get from shared needles? Holy shit." Nathan had lost all his calm and was sobbing on the ground now.

"Ben, Ben. Are you OK? You never take candy from a fucking weirdo in a clown costume in front of a dodgy building again!! You got me!?" Kyle was shaking his head as he took in the place and realized his vision was starting to blur too. He started to feel queasy and sunk to the ground crawling towards Nathan who was crouched into a corner now and feeling his way around.

"Where are we meant to go?" Ben gasped, the room was pitch black apart from the bright red flashing light and felt small, roughly half the size of a shipping container. The room humid with the smell of rotting wood, the effects of the drug made the room spin which made them feel dizzier.

Ben realized he was touching a chain link fence and then noticed he was bleeding, it was a razor wire fence but there was a small tunnel that he could just see in the dark. The room was spinning and he felt violently ill but he knew that had to be the way, maybe there was a way out. "Guys, this way. We need to crawl through this tunnel. Just be careful of the razor wire."

The trio reached the next section, it was a mirror room, of course it had to be a mirror room with more razor wire and they knew they were going to have to distinguish from the real razor wire from the mirrors. The pathway appeared to be shrinking and the reflections of the mirrors seemed to be getting tighter and tighter as the razor wire seemed to be getting closer as the walls felt they were closing in.

Nathan shrieked as he peeked through a tiny gap and saw a figure wrapped in razor wire staring at him through the gap with one unblinking red eye.

"Something is watching us!!! Nope!!" Nathan almost stumbled into razor wire in panic but Kyle stopped him and noticed the figure too.

"It's dead. Someone tried to make it and they didn't get through. Nathan, he's dead. Move. We need to move." Kyle was trying to be strong for the other two, he knew he was the strongest of the three but he was petrified and he was sure that the thing watching them was dead but had no confirmation.

They reached the end of the mirror tunnel and had now reached a strange small room that had spinning blood red walls with actual tendons that looked like torn veins dripping from the walls and the three could only gag. To add to the confusion there were painted round dots on the floor and round balloons that were blocking some of the pathway and razor wire on others.

"Nope. This is a trap! This looks too easy, this has to be a trap." Ben announced and he took of one of his shoes and threw it on a dot and the three watched in horror as razor wire wrapped around it. "Nope. Fuck this. This has to be a dead end."

"Over here," Kyle shouted. He had reached what looked to be a stair case and it led to a small ladder that looked safe enough. "I think we need to go this way, it leads to something, maybe we can get to the roof." The two joined him and Ben who was at the end of the ladder looked down, it looked as if the platform they had been standing on led to an empty void.

"Guys, we need to keep climbing. We can't go back. Look down." Ben shouted at the other two who gasped as they realized Ben was right and they couldn't go back down.

"The ground has to be there again, it can't just disappear, they drugged us, we are hallucinating." Kyle shouted but Nathan wouldn't budge, the end of the ladder was in sight and they could see a bright light. It had to be the exit.

"What the actual fuck!?" Kyle shouted as he reached the top of the building as the other two joined him. They looked down to see a huge slide leading to a huge hippo like inflatable creature staring up at them and though it was inflatable it was breathing as it was watching them. "No!!!" Kyle went to the edge of the ladder but realized he was staring into a void.

The hippo slowly opened its mouth to reveal razor wire, they knew they were going to be forced to slide straight into the razor wire, fall to their deaths or perish from starvation.

ABOUT THE AUTHOR

Natasha Godfrey

Natasha Godfrey is an Australian scare actor, support worker and horror enthusiast who stumbled into the writing world after tumbling down the freelance writing rabbit hole.

Natasha has overcome personal demons to write and publish books on Amazon including Recovering From Self Harm -By a Recovering Self Harmer and Burn that Trauma Bond and as a horror enthusiast is obsessed with horror.

Natasha has also worked with Endless Ink Publishing House and has completed online work through the platform Upwork which was the platform she used to commence her freelance journey.

Writing aside, Natasha is a crazy cat lady, coffee junkie and creative weirdo.

STORY 2
The Telepath

In year 1997, a man named Robert Strauss had intrigued a number of people because of his peculiar skills. He claimed to have the ability to read a person's thoughts and could move objects with his mind.

He was featured in several shows and other forms of media where he effectively demonstrated his parapsychological talents. He was treated as a rare spectacle soon after his introduction, and he was booked for popular programs until he was given his own show.

Robert practically became a celebrity and a brand of his own in just a short period of time. This very small niche that was often frowned upon had always been in the shadows of successful magicians and other forms of illusionists. The few people who managed to market their skills with a positive response are undoubtedly remarkable.

However, those who wish to profit from these things should tread very carefully. Robert Strauss was one of those naïve individuals who pushed his luck and had to learn the hard way.

Witnesses openly expressed their admiration towards Robert. His fans had adored him with tears when he gave some personal facts and histories about them during his live shows.

The highlight of his events was a segment they referred to as 'deep dive' where he would choose someone from the crowd and perform a thorough analysis to the person's thoughts, and he would end it with a heartwarming advice to their deepest worries in life. Telepathy and enlightenment were a perfect formula for Robert to be acknowledged by many.

His work was treated as a miracle and delivered more substance when compared to other gimmicks that were only geared towards pure entertainment. However, the truth behind his unnatural skills was not as phenomenal as they deemed it to be.

Robert's act was nothing but an elaborate form of deception. He was a great actor with a good marketing strategy. Every performance he did since the beginning was carefully planned or staged. The mindreading he claimed to possess was just a process of elimination based on the person's age and appearance, and he would ask a series of open-ended questions while staying within the lines with high probabilities.

It was a common trick for those who posed as psychics which he repackaged and presented in a different form. The so-called 'deep dive' that he only performed in his own show was aided by hired individuals that he planted within the audience prior to the broadcast, and each of them were only paid actors to go along with the segment.

The telekinetic scenes where he moved random objects within the studio were also manipulated by carefully placed strings and magnets. All of these trickeries were effectively masked as he achieved a respectable stature in the industry, but his successful career was challenged when a mysterious man with the same peculiar feats suddenly came to the picture.

During one of his broadcast, another network launched a program with the same nature. Airing at the same time slot with virtually the same premise, Robert's show was boldly contested by an opposing channel in order to gain from its brimming popularity. It was led by a man with a mask which they only referred to as the 'Telepath', and he performed the same skills as Robert's mindreading and telekinesis.

Robert and his producers would have been treated it as nothing else but a copycat, but the nameless man's performance was clearly far better than Robert's choreographed materials. He was taking things right from the audience's hands that were several feet away from the stage, flying them across the room, and smoothly landing them on his palm.

Robert was completely clueless how the Telepath was doing it. Such a stunt was impossible to fake during a live show and in front of a crowd. Furthermore, he also performed Robert's 'deep dive' to several people in just a short period of time.

After a few episodes, the Telepath was gaining more popularity while the ratings of Robert's show was drastically decreasing. He started to utter some bad remarks in the media towards his competition and how the program was only imitating his show, but a lot of viewers were tuning in to the other channel as they realized the significant difference in their level of skills.

His show eventually grew stale since he couldn't think of a way to defeat his competition. He was removed from the prime time slot and was eventually cancelled a couple of months later. Robert Strauss was completely outclassed by a nameless man, and he was no longer as relevant as he was before.

He once approached him and tried to make an agreement for the sake of his career, but the Telepath apathetically replied with his low raspy voice and said that a singer without a voice shouldn't sing. Robert took his simple remark as a display of arrogance. He knew what he meant, and he felt disrespected.

Robert disguised himself and infiltrated the show to see how they operated. Unfortunately, the result of his investigation was not in his favor. He learned that the people who experienced the thorough mindreading from the Telepath were real audiences and not hired actors, and there was no technology nor any form of trickery behind his Telekinetic stunts.

He could not find any flaws to discredit the Telepath's skills. At the time of his visit, a young boy was standing in front of the masked performer. As a special act, he was dared to identify the child's parents amongst the crowd. After a few seconds of complete silence, the boy suddenly levitated off the stage and hovered above the audience.

There was no harness nor any kind of contraption to support him, and yet he was floating so smoothly in mid-air. The boy gently landed in the arms of his parents after flying back and forth for a short while. The studio was drowning with thunderous applause from the enthusiastic crowd, and Robert's eyes remained wide open as he was profoundly astonished by what he just witnessed.

Discouraged and in disbelief, he couldn't wrap his head around the possibility that his opponent might actually be a genuine telepath. An individual who was able to reach the true potential of his telekinetic abilities was unheard of even amongst the community of psychic and paranormal enthusiasts. Out of desperation, Robert had decided to take some drastic actions in order to regain the limelight.

He hired three individuals to disguise as audiences and sabotage the Telepath's live program. One man tried to knock the things off the air during the telepath's telekinetic routine, and the other one was whispering some false rumors in the crowd to ruin the Telepath's reputation.

However, their third accomplice who was supposed to incite some jeering suddenly stopped the guy from throwing a coin to a floating eyeglasses. All confused, he looked at him and saw that he was flustered in fear. His hands were shaking while staring on a blank space right above them.

For some reason, he strongly suggested that they should get out of the studio immediately. They got away before the guards were able to take hold of them, and they met up with Robert to report what happened. Two of them blamed the other guy for their failure, but they were all dumbfounded when he explained what happened.

Right at the moment when he stepped in the studio, he claimed that he already felt a strange presence in the air. When the stunt began, he saw glimpses of translucent threads coming from the Telepath standing on stage. These threads moved like tentacles and carried the items across the room which made them appear like they were floating, and they were passing through each other without getting tangled.

He said that if he didn't stop the other accomplice from interfering with the show, something bad might have happened to him. When he was about to throw a coin to shatter the hovering glass above them, he saw one of the threads wrapping around his neck.

The other two did not believe in his story, but Robert could see in his face that he was genuinely terrified. This new information was far from what he was expecting. He went to the show before and didn't see anything. However, this bizarre news did not hinder his malicious intentions. He came up with a more aggressive plan to bring down his competition regardless of his inexplicable qualities.

Robert Strauss hired a private investigator to find more about the masked man, but not even the crew of their own production knew anything about his true identity. They didn't know how old he was or where he was from. All of his efforts to ruin his competition's career had no substantial results, and so he decided to set his conscience aside and ruin the show as a whole.

He hired an arsonist to burn down the studio and eliminate the program for good. However, even this bold and selfish plan did not come into fruition. When the arson was supposed to occur, a different kind of terror unfolded upon the guilty instead.

Robert was anxious while eagerly waiting for the arsonist's call. He was browsing different media networks for any news about the fire that he was expecting, but there was nothing. He was worried if he got caught or something went wrong with their plan.

Suddenly, someone knocked on his door. Thinking that it might be the arsonist, he hurriedly opened it without hesitation. Chills crawled up his spine as he saw the Telepath standing on his doorway.

Robert instinctively backed away as the masked man casually entered his house. He mumbled when he asked why he was there, but he did not respond to his question and just shut the door behind him. Robert severely underestimated his enemy. He was more than just a psychic with a few tricks up his sleeves.

The Telepath knew all along that Robert Strauss was trying to sabotage him. From the very first time when he came in disguise to watch the show, he knew he was there. All of the interruptions and rumors about him being spread, he knew that Robert was behind it all. He didn't need to touch nor speak to the person in order to read his mind. The moment that Robert and his accomplices had stepped within his range, the Telepath could already analyze their thoughts and emotions.

When the arsonist came at the studio in attempt to burn it down, he was able to detect him immediately. Unfortunately for Robert, he was about to meet the same fate.

No human could possibly reach the level of parapsychological awareness and prowess that the Telepath had, but he was not a human. Robert grabbed a gun from his cabinet and fired at him without thinking twice, but he was completely unscathed.

The invisible threads snapped wildly and whipped across the walls as he slowly approached Robert who cowered helplessly at the corner. He cried and begged while his body was jittering from absolute terror. The Telepath slowly removed his mask, and Robert began to scream at the top of his lungs.

His skin was paper white, and he had four sets of eyes sharply glaring at him. His ears were long and pointed upwards like that of a hound's, and the countless threads that moved like tentacles were the strands of his hair. As he opened his lipless mouth from ear to ear, all that Robert could see inside it was a pitch black hole as if he swallowed an infinite void. After a few seconds, the screaming had stopped.

On the following morning, the maintenance crew saw a gallon of gasoline and some clothes outside of the studio. Nobody knew who it belonged to nor why it was there. Robert's manager came to his house after a couple of days since he stopped answering his calls, but all they saw was an empty gun and his pair of clothes laid on the floor. There were deep scratches on the walls and the ceiling, but there were neither sign of forced entry nor any indication of a crime. They tried to search for him for a while, but they never saw Robert Strauss ever again.

ABOUT THE AUTHOR

Saint Quinn

A writer and an illustrator, Saint Quinn has ghost-written short stories and short novels for starting authors and narrators in various platforms.

With a writing experience of more than five years, he wrote over a hundred stories under horror and science fiction genres.

Saint Quinn's stories often feature bizarre and unconventional creatures instead of popular icons of the genre, and the disparity between normal humans to these original characters are vividly portrayed throughout his stories.

With more attention to depicting helplessness and despair rather than heroic acts of remarkable human protagonists, the horrors of Saint Quinn does not focus in explaining relatable situations but the unprecedented events of terror to the unknowing. As an illustrator, the majority of his artworks are macabre.

Website:

https://www.teepublic.com/user/saintquinn

STORY 3
Half

He loathed it. They promised him a fun vacation, but his father's hometown was in the middle of nowhere. But he couldn't turn away his parents' request. Nana was dying. No one had the heart to refuse precious, precious Nana.

The one thing that kept him there was the woman.

She was beautiful. Deep, pitch black eyes set on her pale, porcelain face Long, black hair cascaded down to her slender waist. As soon as he saw her, he felt his breath catch in his throat.

She had briefly made eye contact, then as quickly as their eyes met, hers had left, glancing at something only she knew about.

That short moment was enough for him. For the next few days he looked for a chance to talk to her. The idea made his chest squeeze so tightly, it was as if he was having a heart attack.

The chance came at an unexpected time. They were gathered around the table, the sound of cutlery being the only noise made between them. Finally, his father's voice broke the silence.

"I'm out of cigarettes."

It was more an announcement than a declaration. He quickly knew what would come next.

"Boy, go get some from the store."

"Oh, please," his mother protested. "It's past nine. He shouldn't be out this late."

"Don't baby him. He stays out longer back in the city."

"The city is different from this little town," Nana muttered in her sweet, shaky voice. "There are creatures who lurk about, playing cruel tricks on humans."

"Not those stories again, mother."

He quickly stood up before the three of them started bickering. Some fresh air would probably do him good.

The store was a ten minute walk from Nana's house. He quickly purchased the cigarettes and made his way back to Nana's house. His eyes wandered about as he walked. Finally, he stopped in front of the woods. He thought he saw something move.

Then there she was.

He saw her gliding into the woods, her long skirt fluttering behind her. The long hem quickly disappeared behind the tree trunks and she vanished as quickly as she came.

His heart beat like a drum.

Nervousness, excitement, and a strange sense of dread intermingled inside him. He clenched his fists, his sweaty palms a clear indication of his swirling emotions. He decided that he would follow her.

He made his way into the woods. It was dark. He remembered that he hadn't brought his phone but it didn't matter. He had only one goal in mind.

He found himself caught in a thicket and he gasped. His voice cut through the silence in the woods. He paused.

It was much too quiet. There was barely a sound save for his own breathing and the rustling of leaves. Back in the house the sound of crickets was clear and obnoxious, but here, there wasn't a single chirp. He looked around, alert.

He saw something move from a nearby clearing. He strained his eyes and saw her.

She stood alone, a ray of moonlight softly touching her skin. She looked up at the full moon with a gentle smile on her face. She looked so delicate.

It was a magical moment and he just knew it was love.

He quietly watched as she looked up at the sky. A soft sigh escaped her lips. She stretched out her arms, as if she was being carried away by some unseen force. Then he heard a strange, splitting sound.

The woman stretched up high, but her feet remained planted on the ground. Then she twisted her body in a way that was humanly impossible. Ninety, one hundred eighty, two hundred seventy degrees... Round and round she went like a grotesque marshmallow twist that was being pulled in half.

In horror, he watched as her body slowly split in two, her entrails hanging out and blood freely pouring into dirt and mud. He screamed, but no sound left his mouth. He could only watch.

Her pale skin turned dark and wilted and thick, pulsing veins jutted out from her sunken cheeks. Rows of sharp teeth emerged from her cracked lips.

The creature in front of him let out a high, piercing wail as fleshy, bat-like wings tore out of her back. Her upper half soared into the sky, trickles of blood dropping down like raindrops.

He ran. He couldn't believe that was real. When he arrived home he quickly left the cigarettes on the table and shut himself in the room. Wrapping himself in his sheets, he convinced himself that it was all just a bad dream.

He told himself that he wouldn't go near her again, just to be safe. But when he looked at her and her eyes met his again, he had pushed all those thoughts aside and told himself that he had simply dreamt the entire thing.

As the sun started to set the following day, he followed her as she ventured into the woods. For a few hours she simply sat. Then, as the sky darkened and the moon rose in the sky, the transformation happened.

Once again, her body split into two with a piercing sound that made his head ache. The wings sprung out from her back. Blood splattered on the ground and he wondered if she felt any pain. But his thoughts were quickly blown away as he watched her fly off and vanish behind the trees.

He stood there, frozen. He didn't know what to do. A few feet away from him was a woman whose waist ended in a stump. He felt his stomach churn when he glimpsed what was inside. Yet he didn't dare run away.

The hours passed like that as he waited for her return. It was going to be morning soon, and he wondered what he was going to find when she came back. But his thoughts were interrupted by a rustle.

Opposite from him, a dark figure emerged from the shadows. The figure crept up near the woman's lower half and dug into his pockets. Then he sprinkled something on top of her exposed half and ran off. It all happened so fast.

It was a strange event and the young man didn't know what to make of it. He didn't have time to think though. Moments after the woman returned. She flew towards her lower half, intending to return. However, she shrieked in pain.

She desperately tried to pick off whatever was on her body, but her fingers sizzled as they made contact with it and she let out a cry of dismay.

It was getting brighter and the woman became more visibly agitated. Soon, rays of light started to appear and the woman's skin began to sizzle. She began to sob and that was when he came to his senses.

He pounced in front of her and quickly dusted what turned out to be salt with his bare hands, ignoring the nausea building in his stomach. The woman was shocked, but there was no time. As soon as he removed the salt, she placed herself on top of her half and in an instant she was as human as he was.

"Why did you help me?" Her voice was cool and quiet, but sweet. Something about it and the way she looked at him urged him to reveal his feelings towards her. It was embarrassing and not the best time, but it looked like she was glad with his honesty.

"You know that I am different. And that I'm not safe."

He nodded, looking at the caking blood in one corner of her lips.

"Still, I like you."

"You may not feel the same way once you understand what I am. What I really need to live."

He insisted that it didn't matter. His feelings were real. The woman sighed and proposed a deal.

"Visit me every night for seven days here, at midnight. If you still choose to stay, I will believe you."

He agreed. That night, he watched as she divided herself once again. He swallowed the bile rising up his throat as he watched flesh and muscle tear away, revealing the bloody contents underneath. Her shriek pierced through his eardrums, and his natural instincts made him want to run, but he kept his feet firmly on the ground.

She flew away only to return moments later, carrying a small pig. She made him turn around, and for that he was grateful. Still, he knew what was to come. Soon, he heard the sound of an ear-splitting squeal and tearing flesh. He listened as she feasted, her lips greedily smacking as she satiated herself.

For the next three days, she brought back prey. Poultry. He remembered back when Nana had shown him how to prepare poultry... all the way from the very beginning. He convinced himself it was the same.

When she was done, there was nothing left but bone. As he helped her bury it, he couldn't help but ask if it was stolen.

"I will die if I do not eat," was her simple reply. There was a hint of annoyance in her voice so he didn't dare to question it anymore.

On the fourth day, it took her longer to return. She had appeared behind him, dropping something with a loud thump. He turned around to see a terrified man gaping at him.

The two stared at each other, equally trying to understand the situation. He looked rough, but the gash on his face and the frightened expression reduced him into a trembling mess.

"A person?" That was all he could ask.

"He is a criminal. He steals. Abuses women. My friend was one of them."

"But a person...!"

"This man is a monster. If we let him live, I will die in his place and he will be left to commit more horrible crimes in his wake. Now, turn around."

He swallowed. The rough-looking man sat bewildered, trying to understand the conversation. Then, their eyes met.

"P-please, please...."

The man tugged at his pant leg. He could feel the fingers spasm. It was a weak hold, but the man's fear and desperation made him hesitate.

"Have you hurt people?"

"No, no..."

"Why did you do it?"

"I... I wanted... I needed money. Everyone does. You understand, right? It was their fault. They fought back. They were just women.

But... Please, please. Help me."

When he heard the man speak, he was convinced. He slowly turned around.

"No! No!"

He heard the sound of ripping fabric. Felt the man's fingers desperately grip his pants, only to be violently pulled away. Guttural screams filled the air until it was finally silent.

She was finished.

"Thank you for understanding."

"He was trash. That's why."

"Because of that, I won't have to feed for two days."

Her voice was appreciative, and he felt her soft, slender fingers touch his hand. That alone made the ordeal worth it.

"There will be one last meal. After that..."

Her voice was sweetly close to his ear, seductive. He shivered.

"After that," he repeated.

He could hardly sleep for the next few days. He didn't have to hear the sound of death, but he longed to see her.

"My grandson appears to be lovesick," Nana laughed. "Introduce her to us next time."

He smiled. That would be nice. Nana would love a girl like her.

The final night came sooner than he thought. He stood in the clearing. When he arrived, she had already split into two and gone ahead for prey.

He looked at the stump before him. Slowly he awkwardly placed his hands on her hips in a makeshift embrace. Amidst the sickeningly sweet smell of blood was the scent of flowers. She was soft and delicate to the touch and it made him feel excited.

"I'm here."

He jumped, letting go of the body.

"I wasn't, I just-"

He spun around, only to meet a familiar pair of confused eyes.

"Nana...?"

His grandmother knelt on the dirt, her body covered with gashes and bruises. She looked visibly shaken, and she stared at him for an explanation. Sweet, sweet Nana.

"My boy, what... what have you done?"

"Nana, I... This wasn't supposed to happen."

He looked at the woman for an explanation, but she remained silent.

"Turn around," were her only words.

"I... This... It's Nana. I told you about her."

"If I don't feed, I'll die. But she... will die soon anyway."

He looked at his frail grandmother. Forgetful, naggy, sweet, precious Nana.

"Nana will understand," she whispered in his ear, her arms wrapping around him. She felt her warm bosom against his back, her breath on his neck.

He looked at Nana and could only think of the past. Nana's signature coconut cream pie. Nana teaching him how to sew. Nana taking him to the mall. Nana buying him candy in secret. Nana on the phone as he ranted about his father. Sweet, sweet Nana.

That's right. Nana loved him very much.

Nana will understand.

He turned around and covered his ears. Still, the screams rang through the night. It lasted so long, and he cursed. Nana was supposed to be weak. But she just wouldn't die. Please, Nana. Let it end soon.

Finally, it was over. He felt her hand swing him around and then he was looking into the eyes of the beautiful woman he loved.

"Thank you," she said, eyes brimming with desire. "You do love me."

She placed her bloody hand on his chest and he embraced her small body. Their faces leaned close and they kissed. He closed his eyes as a wave of bliss filled him. She was soft, she smelled good, and her body was light-

Only he felt no body.

He opened his eyes and stepped back. With a sick squelch her head landed on the ground, right next to the pieces that made up the rest of her body. From a distance, Nana's eyeless head stared at him, blaming.

"Why? Wha... What is this?"

He knelt in front of her pieces, trying to gather them, put them back together. He felt his fingers get tangled. Hair? No, string.

"Why? Why?" He screamed.

The quiet forest suddenly rustled with life. Laughter echoed from the trees around him. He looked at Nana.

"There are creatures who lurk about, playing cruel tricks on humans."

ABOUT THE AUTHOR

Lizzette Adele Ardeña

"Addie" is a freelance content writer based in the Philippines. She works on articles and short story assignments after finishing work at her primary workplace. When it comes to writing, she enjoys horror the most.

Since starting freelance writing in 2017, she has delivered short stories, eBooks, and interactive fiction scripts in various genres. Horror and thriller are her most predominant works.

In her free time, she crochets children's clothes while watching horror movies or listening to podcasts about serial killers. Addie loves potatoes and dairy products.

She currently lives with her family, including three dogs and a cat.

STORY 4
Strangled

Routine checks, routine checks, and routine checks. Walking on the factory balcony, the sheer tediousness of repetitive work made me dazed and uncaring. And in a moment lived in that uncaring nature, the tool bag I was carrying slipped my hand.

Holding the railing with my other hand, I tried to catch the bag from falling to the first floor of the factory, around 5 or 6 meters below me. With all my weight on the railing, everything snapped all at once, and as I lost my balance and fell over the railing, a cable hanging down in a U shape like a snake from a tree branch caught my neck.

Everything on the ceiling rattled, and my legs started swinging around as my hands tried their best to free my neck from the grasp of the cable. I found myself hanging in the center of the factory, meters above the ground. As I gasped for air, consciousness escaped me.

I was in a slightly rundown apartment building. There were two doors per floor, with narrow stairs going up and down. I was looking at the door that was right beside the stairs going up. I didn't know where I was or how I got there. I took a step forward towards the door and coughing like I swallowed the wrong way, rang the doorbell.

I couldn't hear anything at the other side of the door for a while. After some time, the sound of the bolt opening echoed inside the apartment and the door opened slowly.

An old man was looking at me, he was wearing the same clothes that I was wearing. Then, I saw a child, around 10, looking at me from behind the old man. The second I looked at the child, I recognized him. He was me, my younger self. The face of the older man started to look familiar as well when I made the realization.

I couldn't open my mouth to say anything before the old man said "Yes, I am your older self, and he is the young one. Come, help us."

He held my arm and pulled me into the apartment. I was in a small room overlooking a short corridor to the left, kitchen on the other side, and a closed door right in front of me. The wooden door had 6 blurry glass panels etched into the wood to make blurry windows in a 2x3 pattern.

The door handle was thin and rusty, the door didn't belong here. The rest of the house looked modern compared to it. The hall was somewhat dark, with only the light coming from the window of the kitchen barely making its way here. The bright light of the sun coming from the apartment's windows died away as the door was closed behind me. The old man pulled me all the way to the very front of the old door.

"Here it is." The old man said.

I looked at him, and the child, me, standing behind him. It took a few seconds for me to collect the right words to express my confusion "How am I seeing you two? Are you, I mean are you actually here, you two?"

The old man, throwing concerned glances at the wooden door, said "I remember. You choked on the cable, in the factory, right? Yeah, not easy to forget."

"Wha-"

"Look at him." The old man pointed at the child, "He strangled him." Then pointed at the door.

"Him." I said, emotion escaped my gaze. I looked at the door.

"He is in this room, and we can't let him escape." The old man looked around, "I haven't been here long too but at least I know how it ends, right? There should be some planks in the bedroom, you know where it is."

"I don't know." I said, filled with confusion and panic. "How do I know? Where am I?"

"Remember. I know you will. We are in the house. The house."

At that moment, memories locked away slowly came back up to the surface. I looked at the door, so familiar and distant, nostalgic in the most terrifying sense.

My home, my childhood home.

The old man shook my shoulder to make me come back to my senses. I looked tired in my old age. He pointed at the kid and said, "The creature in there, the monster, that thing choked him once, we can't let it happen again."

I rushed to the bedroom. Few wooden planks along with a tool bag was waiting for me there. I grabbed them and made my way towards the hall as fast as I could. The child stood back as me and the old man grabbed the planks and nailed them both to the frames around the door and the door itself. As we did, I started asking questions, lost in my work.

"Why are you two here?"

With slow and methodical words, he said "The kid came here after getting strangled, lack of oxygen. I guess this is the place where we go to."

I looked at him, he didn't look back, and kept working on the nails with his hammer as I held the plank in place. I felt my vision go ever-so-slightly blurry and darker, and there opened a pit deep in my stomach, weighing me down. As I took a weak breath in panic, he then looked at me.

"Yeah, all three of us, we are slowly going."

The sentence reverberating inside my head, I looked at the kid, and motioned him to come closer "Come on, help us." The kid looked scared, I wanted to involve him, but he stood at the other side of the hall, close to the apartment door.

"He is scared. Leave him."

My mind was going physically numb like an arm slept on. The doorframe was filled a good number of planks now, nothing could come out of the living room. As I held my head up to see our overall progress barricading the door, I saw it. A silhouette was standing on the other side, with the glassy windowpanes showing the glassy darkness of the figure.

I took one step back and felt my every being fight to not lose myself to panic and dread, I heard the kid scream behind me, but the old man stood there, looking at the figure on the other side.

I whispered, "It can't get out now.", trying to believe my own words.

"I will protect you." The old man said, looking at the kid, and then me.

I started coughing again. My throat felt like a weight was dropped on it, "Can we do anything else? We should be able to do something more, to keep it out?"

"It's in the house, nothing we can do to keep it out now. We can only contain it in a section."

"I know, that's not what I meant, I-", coughing became a fit as I wasn't able to continue the sentence, I saw the old man's eyes get red as his hands shook. He was coughing as well, and so was the kid. I didn't know what to do, escaping wasn't an option. This was my house.

So, I took a step forward and took the last wooden plank that was laying on the floor and motioned to my older self to help me. He took the plank out of my hands, and pushed it against the door with force, with the impact echoing throughout the empty and silent house. He started to nail the plank in as he said "Look, it will get out. Any time now, really. Don't be scared, fight it. He is just a shadow, a weightless thing, something you can easily push away."

He looked at me with a certain aura of despair and added "It will get better."

That's when the first thump happened. The loud thump came from the other side of the door, and the whole house shook with it. It was a dry sound, accompanied with the cracks of the wooden door. The old, rotten wood wouldn't hold much more impact. Then, it happened again. Like clockwork, every 5 to 10 second, there was a single thud.

We all waited, stepping away from the door, the shadow's agape mouth could be made out from the small windows, it was towering over the door, with only the highest rectangles of windows showcasing his head. Thud, thud, thud. The wood cracked, crumbled, and screamed.

Everything was blurry now, the weight on my neck and head getting heavier every single second. I coughed; every breath was harder than the last. I could see the old man's breaths getting shorter and more distant as well, as he stood a few steps ahead of me, with arms slightly open, in a pose with intent to protect whoever was behind. I looked at him, and then realized I stood similar, with the child right behind me.

"Be ready," The old man turned his head around and looked at me, "door is about to break."

I shook my head at him, which gave my neck even more pressure. My breaths were rapid now, with air coming in and out with a slight whistle, almost a whimper.

Thud. Thud. Thud. Thud.

Thud. The glass broke as the top half of the door fell on top of the old man, and the rest of the door shattered to tall pieces of wood. Pieces flew all over and grabbing one that has fallen at my feet, a sharp one, I ran towards the thing.

When I was only a few steps away from it, the thing looked my way. It wasn't even looking at me, but my general vicinity. It was made of darkness, almost like a living shadow, it had the silhouette of a face, with a mouth agape and eyes distant and cold.

It was looking slightly downwards, with shoulders weak and sloped. It was terror incarnate, such being only fit to live in the dark corners of a room, crooked in impossible positions, and without a single feeling or emotion. Its fingers were long and thin, with a hand abnormally large, followed by dreadfully long arms thin as the piece of wood I was holding. I was stuck in place, frozen in horror. The old man was crushed under the door, but I could still see him breathing.

The thing grabbed a plank that was still nailed to the door frame and crushed it like tin foil. He got over the rest of the planks by getting more crooked and warped, with unnaturally hasty and static movements that echoed blood curdling cracks, cracks akin to bones breaking at every movement the creature made.

He made his way to me, with legs bent backwards. It was denying the space of reality around it, it didn't belong, didn't deserve to be here, every air particle it touched, it corrupted it. I was filled with dread, terror, absolute shock, but also immense anger. Anger so pressurized and uncontrollable, it was able to take control of my body from the shock that kept me in place.

He looked like it felt that I was in control again and upped his pace towards me, and it was right in front of my face in the matter of a second. I raised the wooden plank and stabbed him with it, right on the center of the chest.

It screamed as I gasped loudly for air. It raised its crooked arm with more than one elbow going in different directions and held my neck with unnatural force. In that moment, I felt everything get crushed.

I heard the scream of a man familiar as blood jumped to my brain, my eyes wide open, and ears ringing. One moment later, the hand left my throat for a single moment, and in that moment, I jumped forward, felling the creature and me with it.

My vision blood red and my throat singing a decrepit single note with gurgling, I grabbed a glass panel from the floor. It was broken horizontally in the middle, making up a sharp triangle. With unimaginable ferociousness, I stabbed him, repeatedly, an uncountable amount of times, with the old man holding onto his feet. As I stabbed and stabbed, my vision slowly went and went, only to go away completely.

I heard a loud snap as all the pressure in my neck went away. My stomach dropped and after a moment, I felt a sharp pain in my leg as I hit the ground. Trying to wait for my vision to come back, I gasped, and oxygen filled my body. With air filling my lungs, I looked up, and saw the snapped cable slowly swing on the ceiling.

ABOUT THE AUTHOR

Umut Ceylan

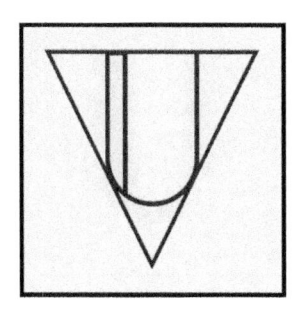

I always look forward to reading, watching, or doing anything with any type of media involving horror and the unknown. From the very tempting and almost glamorous portrayals of the underworld from the start of cinema, from how much we didn't know in the past, and how much we will know in the future, everything can be span into something terrifying to anyone. Being scared, enticed by such visions from the comfort of your couch can be almost cozy, comforting even.

I strive to write about the mysterious of many. My role models in horror include but are not limited to H.P. Lovecraft, Junji Ito, Zdzisław Beksiński, and countless other talents all over the world doing something new and terrifying but enticing and beautiful in their own twisted way at the same time.

I've been writing horror since 2010, starting with Turkish at first, I transitioned into writing in English to reach a wider audience. My goal is to entertain, and invite new worlds into our psyche, thought experiments that scratch that itch at the back of our minds.

See you there.

Other short stories:
https://medium.com/@umutceylan

You can reach me at:
umuthceylan@gmail.com

STORY 5
We All Have Secrets

"How much longer", Alex yells from the backseat with her phone in hand and a disgusted look on her face.

We had been driving for hours at this point, but we were just happy that Josh had planned this trip for us. After COVID-19 and countless other things disrupted the flow of life, we were ready to get back to hanging out as a group again. We hadn't properly hung out together since before the pandemic, but even then, it was hard to catch up with everyone's schedules.

"We will be there soon, I promise', Josh enthusiastically replied to Alex as we make a sharp turn.

Josh had always been a really cheerful character. He was always the jokester of the friend group, full of wit and charm. When he recommended this trip, we were all hesitant, but when he said he'd plan everything for us, how could we say no? So, here we were, in the middle of nowhere, with no reception, finding a spot in the wilderness.

"Surely we will have signal when we get there?", Jess asks without looking up from her phone, trying to get even one bar as Clay, her boyfriend, rolls his eyes at her.

"Uhh, the point of this was to spend time together. I doubt we will get any service out here", Matthew replied in a carefree and almost bored tone as the trees around us become thicker.

We go along for another twenty minutes, but it feels like forever at this point. Finally, we pull into a spot in the middle of nowhere, hop out of the car, and stare in disbelief as we are presented with one of the finest views in the world. Trees, cliffs, and snow-coated mountains in the distance left us all in awe.

Even Matthew, the Debbie-downer of the group, was completely shocked, standing there with his mouth open. For the first time ever, he was speechless.

About an hour later, the sun begins to set, and we begin to grab some sticks and start a campfire. Josh quickly runs into the tent once the fire is going to go and grab the food we planned to cook over the coals.

"Shit!", is all we hear as Josh runs out of his tent empty-handed. We all look up to meet his gaze and he is frowning. "I forgot the food", he whispers.

"Are you serious?" Matthew grumbles in a low tone while burying his face in his hands.

"First, we have no reception, and now we don't even have anything to eat. What the hell are we supposed to do out here?" Jess exclaims.

"I've got a few ideas", Clay winks at her at pulls her in for a cuddle. Clay has always been pretty predictable and driven by his sexuality, so no one is shocked when he says this.

All of us were excited now, but Josh forgetting the food was yet another thing that sucked the fun out of this. We were so far away from civilization that we wouldn't be able to leave until morning to get food. All we had was a 24-pack of beer, a few bottles of vodka, one bottle of tequila, and a 6-pack of water.

This line-up wasn't ideal, obviously. When Josh catches me staring at the booze, he enthusiastically yells "Shots!".

Everyone shrugs their shoulders without the enthusiasm Josh had used and agrees.

"How about we tell scary campfire stories?" Jess suggests.

"Ahhh, pass", Alex breathes out sarcastically.

"How about we play a drinking game?" Josh suggests

"Hell yeah", I say enthusiastically, "That sounds much better than stupid campfire stories!"

"How does it work?", Alex says

"The game is called 'We All Have Secrets'. It goes like this. First of all, a moderator will be chosen. The game starts with the moderator, and then we will go around the circle and each person will tell us a story about a secret they have. You must end each story by saying 'we all have secrets'. If you don't, you have to drink. If anyone believes your secret isn't embarrassing or true enough, the moderator will take a vote. If the majority of the circle agrees, the person has to drink and tell another story."

"I mean, doesn't this count as campfire stories?" I speak.

"Well, with a little twist", Josh says and winks at me. He continues "One of the ways to get around this game is to lie and tell a false story. However, if we catch you out on your lie and you can't prove that it is true, you have to do exactly what you lied about."

"Okay, okay. This is sounding more interesting now", I say as Matthew nods in agreeance.

As I say that, we all turn our heads to look behind us where we hear a crackle in the forest. Jess looks towards Clay with fear in her eyes as Alex gulps.

"Ladies", Clay laughs, "It's probably just a bird."

They all laugh at how stupid their actions must have looked.

All of a sudden, Josh pipes up and says, "Okay, since I'm the moderator, I'll start".

"So, a few years ago, I went to call a girl I'd met at the bar the night before, but she didn't pick up. I left a hungover, half-drunk message about how hot she was and how I wanted to see her again. Soon after, I received a text to meet up. Turns out, I had misdialed the number and the person I met up with was NOT the girl I'd met that night. We all have secrets." Josh says while grinning at us.

"You have got to be kidding!", Matthew almost yelled. At this point, the girls are giggling with delight.

"Shut up, you, guys. Okay, your turn Matthew."

"One time, Alex and I kissed in front of everyone. We all have secrets", he says.

"That has to be a lie", Clay says while looking amused.

"That did not happen", Alex says with disgust.

"Fine, guess I lied. But now, it has to happen according to the rules", Matthew says, clearly amused thinking he had found a loophole.

Josh groans and says, "Moderator discretion, drink and go again." Matthew grabs the bottle, takes a shot, and places it down with a foul look across his face.

"Fine. On time, at work, I shit myself and had to change my pants. When they found the dirty pair in the bathroom, I blamed it on my co-worker. We all have secrets. Your turn Alex." He says begrudgingly.

"Last week, I swear I had an alien encounter. I saw a UFO in the sky. We all have secrets", she says.

"Where did you see this", Clay questioned.

"At my house! From the roof! It looked like it was in town!" Alex exclaims, obviously very proud of herself. "Alex, that would've been the sign for the movie theatre." Clay frowns at her in disbelief.

As everyone laughs, Josh admits that he won't void this one because it was embarrassing for Alex and technically within the rules of the game. Alex sits on her chair with a whole blush taking over her face.

We began this night with such innocent stories. I was hoping someone would soon spice it up with something more enjoyable or sadistic soon.

"My turn", Clay announces excitedly.

"I collect animal skulls at my house. It started when I was young and now it's grown to take over the entire bookshelf in my bedroom. We all have secrets."

"Yikes, pretty creepy. Please go Jess before I actually think too much about that." Josh says.

"Mhm", she slurs. "Well, once I was hooking up with a guy in a club, and I bit his ear. I was drunk and obviously in the moment, because I felt a metallic taste and then swallowed something. When I ran to the bathroom, I had blood on my lips. I think I bit some of his ear lobe off. We all have secrets." I wonder if anyone else is freaked out by how casually she told that story or if it is just me.

"That didn't happen," Clay says. "You have to prove it."

"How am I supposed to prove that? I can't.", she speaks in a confused tone.

"You have to do it!" Matthew adds.

"I guess I volunteer then", Clay winks at her.

She crawls over to him without hesitation, realizing that those were the rules.

I quickly raise my voice and say "Guys, are we actually doing this right now? Maybe we should stop this."

As Jess begins to nibble on Clay's ear, she bites down and he yelps. "Ouch, ouch, okay stop, I get it."

As she pulls away, you can see that she only bit him lightly, but enough to draw blood.

She wipes her mouth, "Your turn, Mikey", she says as she motions towards me.

"Hmm, okay. One time, this guy was bullying my little sister, so I broke into his place and painted 'I'm watching you' on his walls with red paint. He never bullied anyone again. I don't think he even leaves the house much anymore. He's home-schooled now. We all have secrets." I casually say to the group.

"That isn't true. Who was it?" Josh says to me.

"Callum Turner. A guy from my hometown. I don't know how to prove it." I said to him.

"Okay, if you can't prove it, you know the rules. Another story please, good sir." Matthew says.

I didn't know if I wanted to share this story, but with the amount of drinks I have in me at this point, I was full of liquid courage, as was everyone else. They probably wouldn't even remember.

I take a slow blink, swallow my courage, and continue, "My sister and I were being stupid at an abandoned apartment complex once. We were showing each other lighter tricks and I failed one. We set the place on fire. We all have secrets."

"Wait, that was you? Didn't someone die in the blaze?"

I slowly nodded. "I ran as soon as we knew we couldn't put the fire out. We didn't know that there was a homeless woman staying inside. I never told anyone because they thought it was just spontaneous combustion."

"What the hell man", Josh says.

"I don't even know what to think or say", Alex says.

At this point, I looked away from everyone. I was pretty embarrassed. The fire was the only sound drowning out the silence while everyone stared at the floor. I'm really not sure I should've told them that, but I could see everyone around me getting drunker by the second. With hazy eyes, I watched everyone start to wobble thanks to how much alcohol we consumed.

"I'm really not feeling very well", Jess mumbles.

"This is why we don't drink on an empty stomach", Matthew slurs with a slight giggle.

As my vision started to go, I quickly turn to Josh. "Your turn again, my good pal."

Josh nods his head and says "Okay, but one more shot for everyone first."

I think we all wanted to say no, but he was already pouring out more shots for us.

"One for you, one for you, and one for you", he says as he hands the last three out.

"Where's your drink", Clay says.

"I don't want one, but you'll need one for the story I'm about to tell!"

Excited, we all look at him, waiting in suspense.

"Let me just start by saying thanks for coming tonight, guys, it means a lot to me. I've been planning this trip for a long while now, and it's better than I ever could imagine having you all here. You guys really do have a lot of secrets. Now that you are all feeling pretty out of it from the alcohol, I'd like to let you know that I've been spiking your drinks all night and now I'm going to torture and kill you. We all have secrets." He says as I look up at him to see a sinister smile creep onto his face.

"You remember the rules of the game, don't you?"

ABOUT THE AUTHOR

Nikita Hillier

Nikita Hillier is a highly educated professional writer based in Western Australia.

She launched her full-time professional writing career back in 2018 after writing as a hobby and part-time for many years beforehand. She has a strong interest in the mental health, thriller, philosophy, pet, and lifestyle niches.

Nikita works for clients globally to create content that is unique, well-researched, and fuelled by passion. She is the ghostwriter behind several best-selling books and can't wait to publish her own books once they are finished. She is currently working on three different books and hopes to publish them in the coming years.

When Nikita isn't writing, she spends her time studying and gaining more knowledge. You can keep up to date with Nikita via the links below!

Website: https://www.nikitahillierwriter.com

Instagram: https://www.instagram.com/nikitahillierwriter/

Facebook: https://www.facebook.com/nikitahillierwriter

LinkedIn: https://www.linkedin.com/in/nikita-hillier-a66495226/

STORY 6
Filthy Rich Bloodsuckers

"This one's a fighter!! Keep still kid!" One of the men barked into Jacobs ear as he struggled to get free, he was surrounded by six adults and as a skinny young adult he was finding it difficult to fight them off.

Jacob had never been in a fight, had good grades and was devoted to his loved ones and now he was fighting for his life. Jacob had been walking home from his campus after a study session and had been chased into a dead end road by some brutes.

"Please!! Let me go!! Don't do this to me!!" Jacob begged, tears running down his face as six large men surrounded him and all he could see was that they were wearing ski masks and leering down at him.

Jacob choked out a strangled sob as they brandished syringes and plugged it into a tube that was attached to a large empty container. Jacob was a regular blood donor, he donated plasma regularly and had good veins and it dawned on him now that they were literally about to drain him of his blood and he screamed and sobbed as he realized he may not see his loved ones again.

"Please stop this." Jacob sobbed and suddenly the men roughly let go of him and shoved him forwards and Jacob thought they were going to free him so stumbled forwards.

That was when one of them grabbed him and hit the side of his face hard against the cement floor and Jacob winced in pain and his ears rung. He was dazed but aware of the fact they rolled him on his back and stabbed syringes into his arms. "Please." He barely whispered and one of the men spat on him and he sobbed.

Jacob watched in horror as they drained his blood and collected it, his adrenaline made the blood pump into the container faster and Jacob could feel his heart working overtime and was sure he was going to die. Not that these people cared, he was sure that was what he wanted, no one would find him until morning and Jacob accepted his fate.

Jacob woke alone on the street, he was alive but he was unable to move. He was aware of the air and the cold hard cement he lay on but he was drained and his head was spinning, he was freezing and his lips were dried. They had left him for dead but he was alive somehow.

****

The campus was in shock, last they heard a young freshman college student named Jacob had been attacked, rumors circulated that he had been attacked by vampires who drained him to the brink of death.

Jacob had been reported to be a kind, sweet and talented medical student who was committed to his study and since deferred after the attack and become a hermit too afraid to leave his house.

The college since developed a 'safety in numbers' policy and students would leave accompanied at night with other students or if they were alone escorted by security.

Of course, there was always a means to breach the security system and these people had a lot of contacts and a lot of money. The university was bribed to cover up Jacobs assault and students begun to quiet down and Jacob was soon forgotten.

Sally and Ella walked side by side next to the two burly security guards, they were both short tempered and gruff but kept the two petite young women safe.

"Thank you so much for keeping us safe tonight, we have been so scared about these vampire attacks lately. Jacob was a really good kid, we saw him around the campus a few times and he was so nice."

"Apparently there is a rich organization who sold his blood to bidders on the black market and there are real life vampires. We feel so safe with you both, thank you so much." Sally piped up.

"It's our job. The gate to the cars is locked so we need to take a detour." One of the gruff security guards grumbled and for a minute the girls thought they saw the two men exchange a knowing look as they reached the car park.

"You girls want to know something? Your blood is worth a lot of money and we knew Jacob better than you because we were the ones who attacked him." The second security guard said, his tone serious and the girls giggled nervously until both of the men seized them by the hair and henchmen in black ski masks laughed as they ran towards the girls with syringes.

The girls shrieked and were easily over powered by the men. The men laughed in the girls faces as they started begging and pleading for their lives and roughed them up to drain them even faster.

"Mummy..." Ella started sobbing out of desperation as she was drained. Ella had an iron condition and was an anemic, her blood loss would be fatal and she had an iron infusion booked next week. "Please I'm anemic. I'll die if you take any more blood."

"You think we give a fuck?" One of the henchmen laughed and Sally could only watch in horror as her best friend was drained to death. Sally started crying and wailing and the cruel henchmen laughed at her and mocked her tears, giving her face one last shove into the dirt before leaving.

"We will be back for you Sally, can't say the same about your friend." Sally blacked out, the ear ringing in her head and exhaustion from blood loss caught up to her.

Sally woke up some time later, everything hurt. She could barely move, her head was bleeding and the men had ripped some of her beautiful curly hair and bruised her, her veins leaked pale red droplets of blood. They literally drained her dry. She collapsed over Ella, heaving and sobbing as she picked up the phone and dialed the police and ambulance.

Trying her best to give Ella CPR in vain, she had no air in her own lungs or no upper body strength left but she had to try even if it was pointless. Ella's dad was a cop and now he knew something would have to be done about this. Ella's dad loved Sally and would be heartbroken.

"Ella please....Wake up.. Please." Ella collapsed she could not go on and she could only sob with whatever energy she had left as she buried her face on her dead best friends chest.

****

It was late at the campus and Chris injected himself with his daily 600mg of Trenbolone, the stuff was illegal and Chris had been taking steroids from the young age of eighteen. His body had adapted to the strongest steroid substance and he knew it was stupid but he trained hard and ate well, he would take Trenbolone till he died.

Chris was a trained MMA fighter and was bursting with testosterone and had a plan to fuck these guys up. Ella was a dear friend of Chris and he wanted to avenge her and he was prepared tonight, Sally's father was nearby with a few silent members of the force. They were going to put a tracker device on the henchmen's car and Chris was willing to play bait.

Chris didn't think much as he was clubbed over the back of his head, he was used to getting hit and this was all going according to his plan. He wasn't planning on fucking these guys up physically in a fight; that would be too kind. Chris had a better plan, they could take his blood but Chris knew that they wouldn't be able to handle the amount of testosterone in his body.

Chris was a biological student, this stuff genuinely interested him and he lay calmly and smiled up at his assailants as the forced the needles into his veins to collect his blood. He wondered who his blood would be going to and what effects it would have on someone who had never taken steroids in their life.

Chris was unable to give blood because of his steroid use, but he was more than willing to give these guys his blood if it killed them. He was willing to try in the name of science.

"Why's he so calm? Fucking freak." One of the henchmen hit Chris square in the face and spat in his face and Chris winced but didn't respond. They took off.

Chris lay exhausted on the ground and lay on the grass to stare up at the stars. It felt peaceful, he may have been a rough guy but he knew he was going to be OK and watched the henchmen leave in their dodgy black van.

He spied something beneath the black van, it was red and flashing and Chris smiled and gave a slight chuckle as he knew the special forces had succeeded and now the fuckers were in trouble.

****

Sally watched the midnight news report on her phone with her father and the two of them were in hysterics, the politician who bribed the university to stay quiet about the vampire attacks wound up in hospital from being poisoned by steroid overdose.

He was in a critical condition with an elevated heart rate, barely recognizable with extreme hair loss and sweaty acne break outs. To top that off he had respiratory issues and a horrible cough to cough up blood and severe erectile dysfunction.

It was late at night and the two were ready to break into the headquarters to poison the blood bank that the van they tracked took them to. The news had confirmed their suspicion that the elite were preying on college students and ingesting or injecting their blood to stay young, it seemed to be the latest health fad as promoted by celebrities.

They easily broke into the back window, the headquarters was a tiny unassuming abandoned corner shop, they would be able to replace the window and seal it up to not raise suspicion.

There were huge vats of blood groups which meant there were other groups carrying out operations elsewhere and that they demographic may have differed and been covered up. The top of each vat screwed right off a little too easily and they supposed the organization was too arrogant to believe they would ever be exposed or compromised.

They spiked the blood with LSD, laxative and drain cleaner and screwed the top of the lids back onto the vaults and left the facility. Placing a matching window pane back onto the window and cleaning up the damage so it looked good as new. They left and knew it would be a waiting game, they wanted to see who else was behind it all.

****

It was beautiful, obnoxious and corrupt celebrities, Neo Nazi henchmen, politicians and corrupt landlords who owned several properties were dying from explosive diarrhea, tripping on hallucinogenic drugs and dying from poisoning.

The news report suggested that those responsible for the student attacks and for the murder of a few students who did not survive were found to be ingesting blood of youths and were recently avenged by some mysterious vigilantes.

"Sir, how did you come to be in this situation?" The reporter asked an obnoxious and intoxicated man who was being interviewed in the hospital by the press.

"Fuck off, I want to talk to my lawyer, he's a pink unicorn you seen him?" The man replied as his eyes darted around the hospital room. "Where did that dragon go, I want my crayons.''

ABOUT THE AUTHOR

Natasha Godfrey

Natasha Godfrey is an Australian scare actor, support worker and horror enthusiast who stumbled into the writing world after tumbling down the freelance writing rabbit hole.

Natasha has overcome personal demons to write and publish books on Amazon including Recovering From Self Harm -By a Recovering Self Harmer and Burn that Trauma Bond and as a horror enthusiast is obsessed with horror.

Natasha has also worked with Endless Ink Publishing House and has completed online work through the platform Upwork which was the platform she used to commence her freelance journey.

Writing aside, Natasha is a crazy cat lady, coffee junkie and creative weirdo.

STORY 7
Wormwalkers

Ever since I was young, I always had a fear of worms. I'd always take care to avoid taking out the trash, or throw something that is spoilt way before in advance to avoid maggots, and I'd never ever even want to touch anything or be near anything wormlike, even if it's merely inside a screen of a phone. You can see just how much I hate these creepy crawlies, and yet, I'm living a nightmare, my whole body, it's infested with them.

Today, I pulled a piece of my flesh out, as I pinched it, a little worm starts crawling out of me. I pinched my leg, and I pulled a much longer worm like, as if it's a parasite and part of myself. I kept scratching my hands, and each time I do it, I SHRED chunks of flesh that then turn into worms and worms onto the floor, this is my nightmare.

How did it all happen? Well I was out trekking in a jungle. At the time I was researching bugs, I'm an entomologist, and I often collect samples of bugs I see around the wilderness. I studied many insects extensively, and I was often out in the wilderness. However, I didn't make it out as I wanted, instead I got lost for hours and hours.

I tried to retrace my steps, but I couldn't find my way out. Although I was lost, I signaled my Portable GPS to merely contact an emergency rescue, no problem, well except for one. I had no water left, I look into my plastic water bottle and realized it was empty, merely a capful. I was thirsty, so I went around looking for water.

I found some stagnant water by a pond. It was muddy and dirty, I couldn't drink it in that state. So, I merely scooped it up with intent to boil it for purification. However, as I scooped it up with my plastic bottle, I saw what looks like tiny lines inside the water. Immediately I knew that these must be parasites.

I hated the thoughts of these wormlike parasites entering me, but it's standard for me to merely rid of them by trying to boil them, no problem. I poured the water into a makeshift beaker I had, and used my portable Bunsen burner to begin the boiling process, I placed the Bunsen burner and beaker down on the floor, and squatted.

The boiling process seemed to be working fine at first, the water was bubbling up from the heat. But instead of killing the parasites, I was shocked on what happened next, the tiny worms instead began to multiply ridiculously fast, and they grew LONGER. And they were fidgeting and wiggling violently as they multiplied, soon the entire beaker began to be covered by it that it became more worms than water inside it.

I was startled by it, I immediately stood back up in shock, but I didn't run away, that decision would soon be a mistake. Instead I observed it, I looked into the worms multiplying even more. It was disgusting, but I couldn't look away, this was something unique so I had to try to make notes of it. What I didn't realize however, was that somehow, the worms overfilled the beaker so much, it exploded the beaker.

The momentum from such an explosion launched what seemed to be countless of parasitic looking worms into the air, and I was in the direction of it. Soon enough I was covered in them, and I was hysterical. I tried to flick each worm out with my finger, but instead, they were imbedded to my body and skin.

Horror set into my mind, the worms were embedding into me one by one. I was slowly being filled to the brim with worms. Immediately I screamed, for the worms were crawling inside my skin, and inside my body and they were multiplying, I can feel it. The worms that did not enter my body were on the ground, wiggling and multiplying, soon enough the floor near the Bunsen burner was embedded by a pattern of moving and wiggling lines, it was disgusting.

I moved away from the area, but it did not stop my predicament. I was hosting a bunch of worms inside of me, and now we're at the present, where I pulled a worm out of my body. So now what? When I cough, I cough a bunch of worms out of my mouth. Seeing that, it caused me to vomit, and when I did that, I vomited not just puke, but A BUNCH of worms out, and then they feasted on my vomit.

There was so much decay and stench, it startled me and I felt like passing out, but I didn't want to sleep knowing I had worms within me. I tried to perform self-surgery, so I took a sharp pocket knife out from well, my pocket, and dissected my arm just to see what was wrong with me.

And lo behold, as soon as I made a slice, worms immediately started to crawl out. They were small, tiny, as the cut I made was small but they crawled out in dozens and dozens of numbers. My arm was bleeding slightly, but the blood let out was nothing compared to dozens and dozens of worms crawling out of the wound.

I patched up the wound, and a sense of despair was instilled in me. A despair and horror of being a vessel to these worm-like creatures. This is where we are now. I'm not sure what to do, my skin is itchy at the moment, I know they're just crawling around in there, multiplying further and further.

What are they even eating? Are they eating me… no, it can't be. But I feel both feel so hungry and at the same time like I can't eat anything. I'm not sure what they're doing to my body, but I'm going mad at the thought of it, I can't stand this horrifying fate I've been left to.

I screamed, and I screamed loudly, I lost my mind. But then an emergency rescue service team managed to finally find me, there were three of them. I was relieved, but I can't keep them in the dark of my predicament. I decided to tell them my situation, about the worms that were crawling about in me and they should stay away from me.

They were confused of course, one of them, a burly man said "Worms? What are ya talking about? What's into ya?". I coughed out, and immediately I spewed a bunch of worms as I did before, they were shocked, they wanted me to come with them, they knew a way out of the jungle and onto a nearby helicopter.

I decided to accept, I needed help right away for the situation. But as I followed them, I felt weaker and weaker. One of them, a thin man, came to me to help me. But suddenly, I had a urge to vomit. I felt like I needed to vomit at that moment, and so I looked into the man's eyes just as he was bout to pull me up, and then I spewed out my vomit at his face.

Now he's covered in worms, the same worms I have. And they were embedding into him. However, this time it's different, this time I noticed the worms were also covering his face fully instead of leaving the outer body alone. His face was like a mask of worms in seconds, they were eating it off.

The other rescue team members looked on in horror. Besides the burly one, a petite woman screamed the same way I did not too long ago. She pierced the heavens with that scream, so the burly man tried to confront me, I'm not sure what he is expecting from me, but he said "What did you do? What the hell did you do to Isaac?" he didn't dare approach me, I can see his hesitation.

But truth is, I didn't know what I did, that vomit instinct, it was out of nowhere. As he began to show his horror, the thin man, Isaac I believe, was now just a wriggling mess of worms on the ground. His body is not visible, only his clothes remain of his legacy. The rest of the rescue team were once again horrified.

Then, they decided to abandon me, leave me to my fate it seems, the burly one said "Cassandra, let's leave, we'll come back for him when we get help!". I didn't want to be left alone, I didn't mean what I did. I tried to approach the burly one, but instead they immediately tried to distance themselves away from me. Something inside me said, "they must join us".

"Get away, don't come near us pal!" the burly one said. But I didn't heed their advice, I tried to grab the burly one, but he pushed me away with his shoulder and I fell down. His clothes where I touched him had worms but they didn't embed onto his skin, and merely dried up and die.

They wasted no time, they ran as soon as I could get back up. And now once more I'm left alone again, except I'm not alone, I have the worms now. I'm not sure what to do, but I suddenly feel numbness all over my body.

Yes, I can feel nibbling in areas of my internal organs, my heart, my kidney, and even my brain. It felt like there was wriggling within me, no doubt, they're eating my organs. I decided to meditate, and so

I came under a tree, and meditated there. Suddenly, I knew how to count exactly how many worms I had within my body.

Forty-three million, eight hundred and twenty-two thousand, and nine hundred and fifty two. That was the amount I had within me, and it was growing. Soon the worms began popping off my body all over my skin and dropping off to areas where it was exposed, the places where it wasn't exposed like my chest was getting hard to breathe.

In fact, I was not even breathing normally, I wasn't respirating via inhalation and exhalation from them mouth and nose anymore. Instead I felt like the air coming through my now slimy skin. I knew then I had to take off all my clothes just to be able to feel air.

I took off my shirt and pants, it felt much better. I no longer had my private parts, it was gone. I was excreting a large slime on my body, I no longer had much skin, instead it's replaced by mucus, and within that mucus were the worms of we.

Yes, it felt more like family. We never felt anything like it before, although we once feared the crawlers, no longer is that fear applicable. Instead, that fear became a sort of relief of collectiveness. Slowly, but surely, the vessel that we once were became more and more subservient to the will of the many, to the will of the crawlers, and to the will of the worms.

The metamorphosis is closing completion, but as we were walking within the jungles, we noticed a trembling in the ground, we feel it's vibrations. We sense another human within the land. The footsteps were moderately heavy, we feel like it's a good catch.

We thus shambled towards the area of where the footsteps were, and we were glorious all the while. When we finally came to be upon the footsteps, we found the lost human being. They began to scream at us, but we understood not it's words, it seems like we could no longer cohere to any human thoughts.

The poor lost human soul, we thought. It was scared, and it needed to be guided, it needed to be saved, it needed to be recollected. The human tried to run away, but instead we grappled it with our arm that has long reach.

We then wrapped our body like a rope around the human, and began to engulf him like a snake using our collective bodies leaving his head open. He had a fear inside his eyes, eyes that were clearly lost to individuality. Just imagine, what would happen instead if there were no fear, no uncertainty, but instead it joined us?

Yes, that would be a great fate, so we then consumed him into our body, he tried to escape, but every time he moved, it was like quicksand in the body, merely getting closer and closer into our consciousness.

And now, he was gone, part of us now. One consumed many, many more to go. We look into the clear horizons for many more souls to be saved, and just then, a large group of people came onto us, wielding weapons pointed to us so offensively.

We were not intimidated, no, instead we welcome their company. We welcome them into us, and we approached them, they began to ready themselves, and so I was walking towards them, I knew, I had new brothers into my collective. I knew, that they want to be with me forever.

ABOUT THE AUTHOR

Zairol Adham Bin Zainuddin

Hey there, It's me, Zairol.

I'm a guy who likes to write. Why do I like to write? Because writing is easy, look how easy it is to put words like I am doing right now. All I have to do is move my fingers on a keyboard or tablet and words come out. Simple as that.

I have studied commerce, and have taken a keen interest in the medical field, I hope one day to further myself in the field of medicine but as of right now, I'd like to gain some experience in the field of creative, content and copy-writing.

Now aside from talking about me and my dreams, what have I done previously? In terms of writing I made a complex murder story and have made a few guides here and there on certain video games. It's a lot more work than you think, but I enjoy doing it and I learnt a lot from it.

That's all there is of the current, If you want to know more about me, go ahead and message me and I'll shoot a reply. Maybe we can discuss work opportunities and we'll be able to collaborate together.

zairoladham@gmail.com

www.linkedin.com/in/zairol-adham-bin-zainuddin-6a350826b (LinkedIn)

STORY 8
The Living Room

Danny's room was like a Comic Con booth—posters, action figures, stuffed animals galore, wherever your eyes landed you'll find a little green man waving hello. And there he was, the boy himself. Sprawled on his bed with mud caked shoes on, reading a comic book about… well you guessed it, another alien!

"Danny! Come down here and help me bring the groceries in!" shouted his mom from downstairs.

"In a minute! I've got a few pages left!" screamed Danny.

He barely managed to finish the page he was on when he heard, "DAAANNY! COME ON DOWN RIGHT NOW GODDAMMIT!" Danny sighed and dragged himself out of bed, he opened his bedroom door and-

Ran straight into his mom.

Hair pulled back in a messy bun, everything about her screamed 'tired suburban mom'. "Danny! How many times do I have to tell you? What were you doing that was so important you couldn't take the damned groceries out of the car?" she chastised.

Danny's mom caught a glimpse of his comic book on the bed and stormed right in, she picked it up and waved it about, "Daniel Hayes, you are going to be eleven in less than a month, you're too old for this non-sense I tell you!"

Danny stood there wincing, he prayed that his mom won't take it out on his comic books again. Last time she got this angry, she donated a whole box of them to the charity shop.

"That's it!! I'm taking the lot down to the shop!"

Danny couldn't believe it, it's happening again! "NO MOM! NOO! DON'T! I NEED THEM!" he screamed as he clung to her. "Enough I tell you!" Danny's mom only managed to get angrier. She took a pile of comic books from his desk and went storming downstairs. Danny helplessly tried to catch up to her.

"Now Daniel, if you ever wanna see them again, I want you doing all the chores around here this week you understand?" She scolded by the kitchen table. Danny stood there and nodded with glassy eyes, tears started to well up.

Danny's mom realized she might've gone a bit too far this time, "Well go on now, get them groceries from the car!" and just like that, Danny was dismissed. You could say his mom wasn't the most emotionally available of the lot.

He was nearly done taking the groceries out, when he heard it. It was a language spoken unlike anything he'd heard before. Over the hedge, right by the garage, two men were speaking in a strange foreign tongue.

It couldn't have been Spanish, he got enough lessons at school to know what that sounded like. And it couldn't have been Chinese, his best friend Steven spoke Chinese at home and they didn't sound like that.

He peered through the bushes and saw two men, strangers who looked just like him. They stood around with their attention absorbed by what seemed like a mobile phone, except that it beamed out a small rotating hologram planet, like the phones used by space troopers in an alien show Danny watched. Danny let out a small gasp, quickly put his hands over his mouth. "Who's there?" asked the taller one, "You better find out what that is and get on to it quickly!" the shorter one retorted and left.

The taller-lankier stood watch for a while; he caught Danny's eyes through the bushes, and smiled at him. An unnaturally wide smile that made it look like his cheeks might split right open. Danny ran straight into his house, slamming the door to the garage behind him.

He came in to find his mom peeking through the curtains, "Would you look at that, someone finally bought Old Milton's house!", she moved over to show him a big mover's truck had parked in front of the house next to theirs, "It's the aliens! They moved in!" Danny squealed in his head.

"Danny, you done with 'em groceries? What do you say we go greet our new neighbors?" His mom gave him a smile so wide he could've sworn she was colluding with them.

And before he knew it, they were standing in the front porch of the Aliens'. His mother knocked, trying to balance a whole basket full of eggs while doing so. No answer. Danny swallowed his own spit. He hoped no one will ever answer that door, especially not the tall-lanky man.

"Mom," he asked, tugging on the hem of her skirt, "Yes darlin?"

"I don't feel too good, is it okay if I go home?" Too late for that Danny! The Aliens' front door swung open and out stepped…a perfectly happy suburban wife. "The only explanation for this would have to be aliens," Danny thought.

"Well hello there! You must be our new neighbors?" she beamed, everything about her screamed 'normal', too normal, like a TV skit of what normal looks like, "Oh and you brought me eggs too? How sweet of you! Oh you must come in for at least a cup of tea!"

His mom practically dragged Danny into their living room, "Now behave Danny, remember I still have those comic books of yours," she whispered to him. Danny did as he was told and sat on their couch, "The Aliens' couch" he thought.

He looked around, the lanky man was nowhere to be found, but the place was already terrifying enough as it was. Everything was in perfect order, not a speck of dust out of place.

Why wasn't his mom bothered by this? She was genuinely having a conversation with that… that thing??? What could it possibly want? Why did a family of aliens move next to his house of all of the places on the planet? Sitting on his neighbor's couch that afternoon, he made it his life's goal to out them, and to protect the planet from their invasion.

He looked over to his mom, enjoying her tea and cakes with the alien woman, who now stared directly at him. "Oh isn't he a darlin'? I'm yet to have kids of my own, we're newlyweds you see, just got married last Spring," there it was, a hint of that same wide smile the lanky man had.

"Oh he can be a darlin' if he chooses to, spends all his time reading those damned comic books I tell you," complained Danny's mom.

"Comic books! How wonderful! Tell you what? We're having a

yard sale this weekend to clear things out. My husband has a whole collection of comic books, I'll give them for free if he'll help out with the counter!" said the alien woman to Danny's mom, without taking her eyes off of him.

Danny's mom looked at her son who was visibly terrified and shrugged. "That may just do him some good," she said, sipping more of her tea. And the alien woman smiled, so wide that her cheeks nearly split open.

Danny had no idea why his mom didn't find this odd and ran screaming out of there, but he knew that he'll have to brave through that yard sale. It would be his chance to infiltrate their home, and find a way to soil their invasion plans.

On the day of the yard sale, Danny's mom made him wear this ridiculous tuxedo t-shirt to make him look like the "fine-young-gentleman" that he is, she walked him over to the Aliens' and air kissed the alien woman good-by before happily going about with her day, sans Danny.

He watched her go home forlornly, "Some roads are too dangerous that one must walk alone," he thought to himself, echoing a line from his space troopers show.

Come mid-morning, the yard sale was a hit! Guess adults aren't too different from him after all, everyone wanted a piece of the aliens', disguised to look like human appliances as they were. Danny stood as he watched the entire neighborhood eat cupcakes and drink lemonades made by the alien woman, while the lanky alien man greeted everyone with that eery wide smile no one else seemed to mind. And by then no one paid any attention to him, now's his chance!

Danny ducked under the counter and crawled into the Aliens' garage. He went in their garage door and found his way to their living room. Then, he got to work on finding evidence. As predicted everything was eerily exactly where it should be, not a cushion out of place. There's no way people actually live here.

Danny was busy going through their kitchen cupboards when the front door unlocked, and in stepped the lanky alien man. Danny ducked under the kitchen counter, slowly crawling on his knees as the man walked over. T

he alien man went to his fridge and drank some juice straight out of the carton. Danny hid on the other side of the counter, hoping he won't get noticed. It was a scene straight out those alien movies he loved.

"Honey! Won't you help me out here? I can't find Danny and I need some change!" screamed the alien lady from outside. Thankfully the lanky man obliged, Danny slowly crawled around, careful not to be spotted. The man opened his front door and Danny leaned back against the counter side in relief.

But he stopped under the doorway and sniffed the air, "Huh? Human smells really do stick to you," and finally he walked out the door, leaving Danny with his heart pounding.

Danny stepped out and went straight to the fridge, he wanted to check out that juice carton. It didn't look like any other he'd seen either. Just as he thought, the carton had alien inscriptions all over. That should be enough proof for now! He was about to sneak out the back door when-

He saw a full scale mirror they had leaning by the stairs. It emitted

a strange glow, like static TV. But when he stood right in front of it, he saw that it was just any old mirror. He saw Danny, a ten year-old-boy in that ridiculous tuxedo t-shirt, holding the strangely labeled juice box. And then he smiled, a smile so wide that his cheeks might split right open.

Danny was horrified, he definitely wasn't smiling, only his reflection was. He wanted to run out the back door but his legs felt like they were glued in place. He realized it wasn't just his legs, he couldn't move his entire body!

He stood frozen in place, panicking, every inch of him tried to run. Slowly the room started to change around him. Blood oozed out of the floors, its perfectly painted walls now matched the color of his skin. Everything around him was turning into flesh! His flesh! Duplicates of his face smiling eerily appeared everywhere around him, on the walls on the couch, on the ceiling!

Everything was made of Danny. The real Danny was slowly being absorbed by the room, he felt like he scraped his knee over and over again. The pain was coming from everywhere. His skin peeled off, his muscles and bones broke apart. He was being diffused into the wooden floors.

In his panicked state, he glanced over to the mirror and saw that his other self was breaking free from the glass. He saw its eery smile staring directly at him as lost control of his body completely, the strange juice box fell from his hand, and everything went dark for Danny.

Come lunchtime though, he was right where he should be—at home, with his mom. It was a rare afternoon where she was perfectly content, having spent the morning without his clingy good-for-nothing son. So she made him his favorite, spaghetti with a lot of cheese. When he was done, he took all the plates and cutleries and washed them thoroughly in the sink without being told to do so.

"Wow! Hanging out with the new neighbors really did miracles on you!" teased his mom.

"I think they're okay, is there anything else I can help out with mom? If not I'd like to go back to their house and help them close up," said Danny, the perfectly normal not-so-human boy.

ABOUT THE AUTHOR

Pia Diamandis

Pia Diamandis, (Jakarta, 1999) is a horror screen and fiction writer who sometimes doubles as an art curator. After finishing her Art History studies in Istituto Marangoni Firenze, she now works as assistant to horror/action film director, TimoTjahjanto - https://mubi.com/cast/timo-tjahjanto

From time to time, she will write film & art columns for online media like Tirto.id - https://tirto.id/author/piadiamandisutm_source=tirtoid&utm_medium=lowauthor and the Gen-Z culture collective, Broadly Specific - https://broadly-specific.com/author/piadiamandis/

She has co-curated an exhibition for Museo Salvatore Ferragamo (2022), performed as assistant curator for the Forme Nel Verde - https://www.formenelverde.com/ outdoor sculpture festival (2018), and worked as a consultant for state museums in Jakarta (2019 - 2021).

While in terms of scary things, she enjoys all things gore and creature horror, particularly those rooted in local lores that are set in current times.

You can find her on instagram @pia_diamandis

Or check out her full portfolio at https://linktr.ee/Pia_diamandis

STORY 9

The Red Room

Josie was getting restless, it was ten o'clock at night, her family were asleep and she was getting sick of studying. Times were tough, Josie had recently broken up with her boyfriend and moved back in with her parents to complete her Physiology course.

She was only twenty four years old and had a natural curiosity for the limits that the human body could take under extreme physical and mental stress. She was ashamed of these curiosities and had questioned her sanity and character for being interested in reading about torture and its lasting effects on the human body and mind.

She had two more years to go and she planned to specialize in the link between the mind and the body for pain management, to have understanding of chronic pain and conditions she needed to research it. She was curious about how she could use her ideas and passion to improve the lives of her future clients, she wanted to learn about exercise, neurons in the brain, nerve pain and therapies.

Josie was finding it hard to study, she couldn't process anything academically and it was time for her to explore the weird site of the internet. She found herself researching long lasting effects of torture on the human body.

She knew she probably had some type of morbid fascination she needed to address but she was curious how others could find it in themselves to torture a human being. She wanted to understand how pain and trauma in the body caused lifelong pain, damage and reduced quality of life. It was incredible what the human body could withstand and how much the human body could tolerate without breaking, though there was always a point where something was going to break and Josie often wondered whether it was someone's mind or body who broke first.

Josie found herself reading about torture methods used throughout the ages, the amount of props, equipment and barbaric inventions which were created to inflict pain, punishment and severe damage on people for several reasons were terrifying.

A warning message popped up on the bottom left of her laptop screen warning her that she has accessed disturbing content and that there may be ramifications or future investigations into her web search history.

Josie hastily shut the tabs she had open and disconnected her VPN, her parents would be furious if they learnt about some of the things she had just been reading it. The message had been a warning and her parents had turned on restrictions and warnings to stop her teen aged brother accessing adult material.

None of her family members knew about her dark interests, she was afraid and had to breathe through her anxiety. She wasn't sure if any action would be taken against her or if the warning had been a one off.

"OK..." She muttered to herself under her breath and remembered hearing a guy in her class talk about a browser called Tor that was used to access The Deep Web. Josie installed Tor, there was something so exhilarating about reading material that she shouldn't and outsmarting her younger brother and keeping dark secrets from her parents.

She had heard rumors of crazy things on The Deep Web that are only accessible on Tor, things which were dangerous and weren't legal.

Her heart raced as she navigated the browser, it was like what she already used but different. There were more things she could research and no filter, no warning messages. She started to research the pages that she had shut down and a suggestion box appeared at the top of her screen.

HOW MUCH PAIN CAN THE HUMAN BODY TAKE- FIND OUT HERE

Josie's eyes widened, perhaps Tor used algorithms and suggestions based on her search history but this temptation was too much for her to ignore and she clicked on it. It was essentially an essay on documentation of torture and acts of violence and cases of illegal and unethical testing on humans but this was exactly the kind of thing she was curious about.

She had read two pages when a bright red box had popped up aggressively on her screen and had taken up most of the screen room on her laptop.

BASED ON YOUR SEARCH SUGGESTIONS... WE WOULD LIKE YOU TO JOIN OUR RED ROOM...

Josie breathed excitedly, she had heard about Red Rooms but never thought they were legit but they were something that fascinated her. Without giving much thought to the consequences she clicked the YES button with her cursor.

An agreement popped up on her screen and she didn't read the fine print, she was too excited and she proceeded to the very bottom of the page to tick the agreement box.

A quiz opened on her screen and asked her to click Male/Female and age, Josie assumed she had to enter her own details so clicked Female-24. A live video of a terrified young woman of her age appeared on the screen, her eyes wide with real fear and her eyes were black with teary mascara.

She was seated in a cruel looking metal chair with metal cuffs cutting off the circulation to her wrists and ankles and she knew the woman was no actress, she was truly being held against her will.

"Holy shit. No!! No!!" She started to panic as she watched the woman in horror as her torturer stepped into the screen and leered at her. All she could see of him was that he wore a business suit but had his eyes blacked out by war paint.

Her eyes darted around in panic as torture suggestions appeared on the right side of her screen and the most sickening group chat that had suddenly been added to her mobile phone. She had been hacked, her personal data compromised and the life of an innocent woman was now in her hands, she was not going to forgive herself for this.

"Hello Josie, thank you for joining. What morbid curiosities would you like to test on your subject today?" The torturer addressed Josie through the screen and she turned her head away to violently vomit as her web-cam activated itself to capture her terrified reaction.

She had never shared her name with the site and she hadn't entered any information anywhere. This could not be happening! This had to be a hoax. "You read the rules Josie. You kill her or there will be severe consequences for you."

"No!!! I am so sorry! I don't want to kill her!! Please let her go!! I won't tell anyone." Josie could only beg, she watched as the torturer circled the terrified young woman and traced a razor blade to the woman's sensitive ear. The woman was screaming and crying and Josie desperately tried to disconnect from Tor but her screen was stuck on the horrible live video.

She reached for her phone to call the police, to take photographs of evidence to hold these people accountable but to her horror the group chat was frozen on her phone.

Josie tried to forcibly shut down her phone, crouching in horror beneath her computer desk and cradling her head in her hair as she dry heaved in fear. She risked a look at her phone which had restarted to play another threatening message across her screen.

DIDN'T YOU READ THE FINE PRINT JOSIE? WE'VE COLLECTED YOUR DATA, PERSONAL INFORMATON AND CREDIT CARD INFORMATION. IF YOU DO NOT PROCEED WE WILL EMPTY YOUR FUNDS, WE WILL SEND THE POLICE TO ARREST YOU FOR ACCESSING A TORTURE SITE AND YOUR CAMPUS AND FAMILY WILL BE INFORMED ABOUT WHAT A SICK PSYCHO YOU ARE. =)

The message was followed by a smiley face which added another element of cruelty that Josie could not comprehend. She screamed into a pillow, hot tears running down her face as she realized no matter what she did she was screwed and she couldn't save the woman. Her choices were either forfeit and ruin her entire life, be imprisoned, be bankrupt and exposed to her entire campus, family and friends and to be blackmailed by a group of sadists or to take the life of an innocent woman.

"Shit...shit...shit..." Josie hyperventilated as she rocked back and forth under her desk. She watched in horror as screen shots of her search history were being added to her social media pages right before her eyes. "No!!! Please!!"

YOU KNOW WHAT YOU NEED TO DO. STOP IGNORING US. YOU HAVE FIVE MINUTES.

"Mum... Dad... " She howled, she could hear them both snoring as they were fast asleep and she didn't dare get her teenage brother involved. He was too young to see such disturbing content and experiencing it in any way would scar him for life. She had to deal with the consequences herself and pray her family and loved ones would understand.

She sat at the computer. "Empty my funds, just do it. You've already won. Please just let her go." She watched in horror as the woman was being threatened by the torturer again, she wasn't being harmed but the torturer seemed to be enjoying their mutual anguish.

"You really think we would ask for permission? We emptied your funds five minutes ago. Now what's it going to be?" A second torturer joined the first and he was holding a Mace with vicious spikes.

Josie could only sob in horror and fear and she couldn't look away in time as she violently vomited a second time from the anxiety and intense situation. She wiped at her mouth. "Please, I won't say anything...." She begged.

"Kill this girl right now or it's over for you." The first torturer growled and Josie could only gasp at the way the man's eyes seemed to glitter in such a cruel was through the screen. He looked so evil beneath the makeup, he looked demonic and cruel. They both did and resembled the types of predators that Josie always envisioned would experience pleasure from working in a torture chamber.

Josie looked at the torture and death options in horror, she could not put another human being through this and slumped to the ground and could only cry loud and broken sobs.

Her phone buzzed one last time and Josie stared at the text on her phone in horror.

FUCKING PUSSY. ENJOY PRISON. XOXOX WE KILLED HER. =)

Josie felt the room spin, her eyes were sore and bloodshot, her nose runny and she had a violent migraine, her ears rang violently and her vision turned to black as she passed out.

****

Josie was numb as she sat in the police car with her head lowered as tears spilled from her eyes, she was cried out and she knew she had effectively fucked up her life in one night. It was midnight and her family had already been filled in by the authorities and they didn't want to see her.

"Hey, you can talk." One of the cops turned to Josie and offered her a reassuring smile as the other drove on, watching Josie in the rear mirror. For a moment his eyes looked familiar and she couldn't place where from.

"I have evidence on my phone, these…these people they were torturing a girl!" She blurted out. "I have messages from them!"

"You haven't got any evidence on your phone."

"Yes I do! You can lock these guys up!'' She pleaded them. The driver turned to face her and she caught a glimpse of stained black make up around his eyes. He laughed a horrible laugh and her blood turned cold.

"Fucking Pussy. Enjoy Prison.''

ABOUT THE AUTHOR

Natasha Godfrey

Natasha Godfrey is an Australian scare actor, support worker and horror enthusiast who stumbled into the writing world after tumbling down the freelance writing rabbit hole.

Natasha has overcome personal demons to write and publish books on Amazon including Recovering From Self Harm -By a Recovering Self Harmer and Burn that Trauma Bond and as a horror enthusiast is obsessed with horror.

Natasha has also worked with Endless Ink Publishing House and has completed online work through the platform Upwork which was the platform she used to commence her freelance journey.

Writing aside, Natasha is a crazy cat lady, coffee junkie and creative weirdo.

Thank you so much for purchasing my book!

If you have the time, it would help me a lot if you could leave a review or just rate my book.

Printed in Great Britain
by Amazon